Tortuga
(Turtle Island)
Pirate Stronghold

Wreck of
Santa Maria

Cap-Haitien

The Citadel

Limbé River

Marmalade

HAITI

Artibonite River

DOMINICAN REPUBLIC

Port-au-Prince
capital of Haiti

OF HAITI

Trotwood

Dr. Pignewton

Fly-girl Betty

Sgt. Ovett   Louie Lapink

Wrigley Slugfest

Tap Tap

Kernel Gluepots

Miss Baba
IN

THE CARIBBEAN FOULBALL CAPER

Written by
Richard Pels & Winslow Pels

Illustrated by
Winslow Pels

A CALICO BOOK
Published by Contemporary Books, Inc.
CHICAGO · NEW YORK

LIBRARY OF CONGRESS
Library of Congress Cataloging-in-Publication Data

Pels, Richard.
The Caribbean foul ball caper / written by Richard Pels & Winslow
Pels ; illustrated by Winslow Pels.
p.   cm. — (The Miss Baba adventure series)
Summary: Miss Baba, a pedigreed poodle and amateur detective,
journeys to the jungles of Haiti in search of
missing friends and a baseball smuggler.
ISBN 0-8092-4482-9 : $13.95
[1. Mystery and detective stories.   2. Dogs—Fiction.   3. Haiti—
—Fiction.]   I. Pels, Winslow, 1947-   ill.   II. Title.
III. Series.
PZ7.P366Car   1988   88-19460
[Fic]—dc19   CIP
                                                                 AC

A Calico Book
Published by Contemporary Books, Inc.
180 North Michigan Avenue, Chicago, Illinois 60601

Design by Gloria Priam
Library of Congress Catalog Card Number: 00-00000
International Standard Book Number: 0-8092-4482-9
Manufactured in the United States of America

Published simultaneously in Canada by Beaverbooks, Ltd.
195 Allstate Parkway, Valleywood Business Park
Markham, Ontario L3R 4T8 Canada

The Caribbean Foul Ball Caper

Cast of Characters

Miss Baba Furbelow: A Briard College graduate with a degree in education. She inherited her old, rambling house in Balston Spa, New York, from a former employer. Besides being a take-charge sort of poodle, Miss Baba was also blessed with good looks, and it was no surprise when she won the Miss Potato Print beauty pageant. With the winnings she decided to turn her Balston Spa estate into Miss Baba's Animal Academy, providing a quality education and upbringing for forty-seven foundlings. Somehow, she still finds time to write the famous "Dear Miss Baba" advice column, syndicated in newspapers around the country. And she's also rather good at solving complex and difficult mysteries.

Trotwood: Miss Baba's playboy cousin. He has an appetite for high adventure and frequent snacks. Educated at Eaton, he developed a passion for fishing, sailing, croquet, fencing, and dining. He can be a real asset in a tight situation. Trot has a quick mind, a big heart— and a host of interesting friends.

Fly-Girl Betty: The great-great-great-granddaughter of Amelia Airdale, the pioneering woman pilot, and a pilot of renown in her own right. She flies the famous Tiger Moth. She and Miss Baba are old school friends.

Amanda & Amonya Teasedale: The setter sisters of Overlook, a once splendid, now dilapidated estate next to Miss Baba's Academy. Their family was once wealthy, but now the sisters rely on the proceeds of Amonya's health food restaurant (The Salad Seminar) and the Poetry Workshop.

Harriet & Leonard Westdale: Sister and brother-in-law of Amanda and Amonya. Harriet and Leonard moved to Haiti to run a baseball factory they had purchased.

Hairy Martha: One of Miss Baba's best students. Besides being very good in engineering and mathematics, she can hit home runs better than any of the other foundlings—that is, when her hair doesn't get in her eyes.

Kernel Gluepots: A retired military man (whose moustache got shot off in the war) and captain of *La Mouche*, a versatile little boat. He is an expert guide to the local customs and geography of Haiti.

Tap Tap: Gluepots' loyal assistant. His mother, a Haitian, named him after a taxicab. He is surefooted, can lift enormous weights, and, though he is very quiet, has an extremely quick and analytical mind.

Wrigley Slugfest: The superstitious little foreman of the Westdales' baseball factory in Haiti.

Livre Overt: The sergeant in charge of the Cap-Haitien Police District, the north part of Haiti that includes the town of Marmalade where Harriet and Leonard Westdale had their baseball factory. He's a member of the Solenodon family.

Louie Lapink: Police Captain of Marmalade.

Nurse Pincher & Animal Maria: The mainstays of Miss Baba's Academy. Nurse Pincher sees to it that the children stay healthy. Animal Maria makes sure the children are well-fed. She's rumored to have a crush on Dr. Pignewton.

Dr. Francis Xavier Pignewton: A quiet, unassuming, but very resourceful scientist. He has invented many useful items, not the least of which is Trotwood's favorite bubble mix.

No sooner had she begun reading, than Miss Baba heard an unmistakable crash...

1

Foul Play

Miss Baba Furbelow, director of Miss Baba's Animal Academy, collected her newspaper and her cup of cocoa and went out on the large, shady back porch. She had started the Academy some five years earlier in beautiful Balston Spa, a small town with a shoe factory, in upstate New York. It was devoted to the care and education of forty-seven homeless orphans. (Actually, once Miss Baba adopted them, they were never homeless again.)

That morning, the children had already eaten breakfast and were busy with their studies or trips to the museum, or they were out playing baseball. In fact, there was a small group playing ball in the backyard.

Miss Baba put down her cup that said "#1 HEADMISTRESS" on it in big, red letters, dabbed the cocoa froth from her moustache, and opened her paper. But no sooner had she begun reading an interesting article on edible hats, than she heard the cry, "Foul ball!" followed by the unmistakable crash of breaking glass.

Miss Baba set off paw-in-paw with the guilty-looking Martha...

Hairy Martha, one of the better power hitters on the Academy's baseball team, had hit a foul ball over the hedgerow and across the neighbor's backyard. The ball sailed directly through what had been a beautiful floor-to-ceiling stained glass window in the house next door.

Miss Baba sighed. She set aside her newspaper and straightened her egg hat. Then she set off, paw-in-paw, with the guilty-looking Martha to the old mansion, called Overlook, to survey the damage.

There they found Amanda and Amonya Teasedale, the gracefully aging sisters whose family had lived in Overlook for generations. Amanda, the older of the two, was sobbing loudly, hunched over a damp handkerchief. Amonya, the proprietor of a health food restaurant and poetry workshop, was usually very optimistic, but today she was no more dry-eyed than her sister.

Martha felt even worse when she saw how upset the sisters were. Miss Baba began to offer apologies. "Your beautiful window . . ."

Amonya waved the subject of the window aside. "It can be fixed, my dear. What distresses us is this." She handed Miss Baba a letter.

The Teasedales' third sister, Harriet, and her husband, Leonard Westdale, lived in Haiti. Leonard owned a baseball factory there in a town called Marmalade. In fact, his factory had manufactured the case of balls Amanda and Amonya had given the kids next door. (This case included the ball that lay on the floor now, in a pile of stained glass.) For weeks, Amanda and Amonya's letters to the couple had gone unanswered. Now this.

The letter was from a Sergeant Livre Overt in Cap-Haitien. He was the police officer in charge of the district in which Marmalade was located. The tiny handwriting on the letter said the Westdales had disappeared.

"Disappeared!" said Miss Baba as she read on. Sergeant Overt said he had been in constant contact with the local police in Marmalade but nothing had turned up. However, some local residents had said that Harriet and Leonard had been taken to the "Land Without Hats." It was a place from which, according to legend, no one returns. He said that he was very sorry about the whole matter and that he would continue to do whatever he could.

"If you don't mind," said Miss Baba to the weeping sisters, "I would like to show this letter to my cousin Trotwood. He knows something of the tropics."

Miss Baba called Western Union. She barked out two short, to-the-point telegrams—one to Trotwood and another to her old school friend, Fly-Girl Betty.

Amanda and Amonya brightened up a bit when they saw that Miss Baba was taking charge. She was a take-charge sort of poodle.

Trotwood was ice fishing in Viscount Melville Sound in the

Amonya waved the window aside...

vicinity of the North Pole. He had left word where he would be, and Western Union somehow managed to find him.

The telegram to Fly-Girl Betty caught up with her in Cheesequake State Park, in New Jersey, where she had been working around the clock air-lifting Red Cross supplies to the victims of a recent quake. She was a very gifted pilot and a Briard College classmate of Miss Baba. Betty's great-great-great-grandmother was Amelia Airdale, the famous, record-breaking pilot. Flying was in her pedigree.

Meanwhile, Martha had arranged the pieces of stained glass on the floor. They were laid out in the shape of a large flower pot with brightly colored flowers. Luckily, only a few small pieces were shattered. Two large pieces were broken in half, but the window could be reassembled. Something told Martha that getting Leonard and Harriet Westdale back safe and sound might be considerably more difficult.

Luckily, only a few pieces were shattered...

Trotwood sat back in his red velvet overstuffed chair...

2

The Game Plan

The following afternoon everyone agreed to meet in the library of Trotwood's house, a sprawling old mansion just down the road from Miss Baba's Animal Academy.

Trotwood sat back in the red velvet overstuffed chair under the imposing portrait of his great-great-grandfather, Captain Biff Wellington. Wellington was known primarily for an invention that revolutionized modern warfare: the portable, military field kitchen. It was often said that Trotwood took after old Biff, having inherited his penchants for high adventure and frequent snacking.

Trot adjusted the cuffs of his crisply starched shirt for the hundredth time so they stuck out just a little, the way he liked them. Deep in thought, he reached for his big droopy pipe and put it in his mouth. He pulled an engraved silver canister from his pocket and unscrewed the top. From it he poured his own special blend of bubble mix. Then he commenced absentmindedly to blow large bubbles in a steady stream. Some of them settled on a highly polished mulberry writing desk next to Betty. She was just about to express her annoyance with Trotwood's habit when the library doors opened and Miss Baba walked in, the Teasedale sisters in tow.

"Thanks for returning on such short notice, Betty, Trot," said Miss Baba gratefully. Trotwood wasn't sure if he was happier to see her or the egg on her head. He had missed breakfast and lunch while traveling. And he had long ago eaten the contents of his briefcase, a blueberry pie sandwich and a plain donut.

Miss Baba quickly recounted the little she knew about the disappearance of Harriet and Leonard. The conclusion seemed clear. "If we want them found, we have to go to Haiti ourselves," she said. Betty was one step ahead. She had already finished computing the course for the flight.

Nurse Pincher and Animal Maria, the round, stubby cook, were put in charge of the Academy. Hairy Martha, who was also a whiz at fixing engines, was asked to go along. She accepted immediately.

Miss Baba then gave special instructions to a few of the children about getting to ballet lessons on time and not playing practical jokes on Animal Maria, and so on. When she was done, Fly-Girl Betty, bristling with excitement, said, "Well, the old Tiger Moth is as ready as she'll ever be."

Trotwood, meanwhile, took care to collect a few supplies — not the least of which was a special blend of bubble mix that Dr. Pignewton, the famous scientist, had created on short notice as a special favor.

Betty checked the gauges and the compass, and they climbed in, waving farewell to the sisters, the children, the nurse, and the cook. Looking over her shoulder, Miss Baba remarked how Betty's Tiger Moth did only minimal damage to the landscaping. Only one of Trotwood's prize rose bushes had been decapitated this time. "Betty's flying is getting better all the time," she thought with a small smile.

They followed the eastern seaboard of the United States, down

along Florida, over the beautiful string of islands that make up the Bahamas, carefully avoiding being shot down over Cuba. Miss Baba had thoughtfully brought along biscuits and cocoa. Somehow she not only managed to serve them hot, but also to keep some semblance of order on the cramped Tiger Moth.

The island of Hispaniola (the western half of which is Haiti) was a land of contrasts from the air. Beautiful, lush forests (the few remaining after colonial times) were surrounded by desolation. They flew over expanses of dried-out brush and bramble and shriveled-up trees, interspersed with green farmlands and swollen rivers that emptied into the Caribbean Sea. The plucky little Tiger Moth followed the coast to the northernmost city of Cap-Haitien.

Beneath them, they could see men pulling loaded carts and women carrying huge stacks of everything from fruit to laundry on their heads. The streets were lined with crude stone buildings, the legacy of the tyrant Henri Christophe. A hundred and fifty years earlier, he had burned the city to the ground. It was rebuilt entirely with stone to prevent it from ever being set ablaze again.

They landed at the Cap-Haitien airport, a small field with a tin shed for a control tower. Miss Baba and Trotwood took their gear out of the plane and bid Betty and Martha farewell. The plane took off again for the island of Tortuga, ten miles to the north. Betty knew the owner of the airfield there. She and her assistant would service the old Tiger Moth for the return flight.

It was close to evening, so Miss Baba and Trotwood decided to check in...

3

The Hotel Crapaud

Miss Baba and Trotwood managed to find a taxi. It was a small open car with brightly colored paintings and sayings all over it. It followed the bumpy, pothole-filled road into the center of town. There it deposited its passengers in front of the Hotel Crapaud, a white-washed stone building that towered over the surroundings.

It was close to evening, so Miss Baba and Trot decided to check in, unpack their bags, and try their luck in the restaurant on the hotel's veranda.

Miss Baba had a new fried egg sent to her room and positioned it carefully on her head. Trot enjoyed an appetizer of several blueberry pie sandwiches while changing. After freshening up, the two adventurers met in the restaurant.

Miss Baba sampled the seafood salad and washed it down with a cup of hot cocoa. Trot, on the advice of the waiter, ordered the house specialty, the Crapaud de Mer, which the waiter said was sometimes called mountain chicken. Throughout the meal, Trot-wood was haunted by the strange thought that the dish tasted as he imagined a toad would taste—if he were ever crazy enough to eat a toad.

Throughout the meal, Trotwood was haunted by a strange thought...

As Trot's meal disappeared, the maître d' came over smiling. "Ah, monsieur!" he exclaimed, "So you enjoy the famous Haitian giant toad just like a native. Very good, monsieur! You must try our ant larva stew if you like this!"

Trot smiled the kind of smile someone makes just before he faints. He deposited the remaining mouthful discreetly in his napkin after the maître d' walked off. Miss Baba said, "Trot, you never told me you had a penchant for toad. Why, I can whip up a toad or two in béarnaise sauce the next time you come to dinner in Balston Spa." Trotwood didn't appreciate her comments, not with a fresh toad sitting in his stomach—and none too peacefully at that.

Trot excused himself from the table to, among other things, buy provisions for the trip. Miss Baba summoned the maître d' once again. "Yes, madam, how may I be of service?" he asked. Miss Baba placed a ten-gourde note in his paw and asked if he could point out anyone who would have a boat and might serve as a guide to take them up the Limbo River to Marmalade.

The first fellow the maître d' suggested came over. He bore a striking resemblance to the maître d' (this, Miss Baba decided, probably wasn't a coincidence). This fellow introduced himself as Henri. He had a smile like a Siamese cat, which

Miss Baba found attractive but hard to trust. Henri asked for a thousand dollars to get to Marmalade, saying it was a very difficult journey. Throughout the entire conversation, he stared at her egg hat and drooled a bit from the side of his mouth. Miss Baba had had enough of this. She thanked Henri with a "don't call me, I'll call you," and signaled for the maître d' again.

"Yes, madam? I trust Henri proves satisfactory?"

"As a matter of fact, I think I'd prefer someone, er, a little older," said Miss Baba tactfully. She suspected, quite rightly, that this Henri pipsqueak was related to the maître d'.

The maître d' cringed a bit, then pointed to a table in the corner. "Well, that fellow over there has a boat. Kernel Gluepots is his name. He is a very famous military hero. It's a shame his boat's not as nice as Henri's, though."

Gluepots was sitting by himself. His feet didn't quite reach the ground, so he slipped off the chair, straightened his feathers, which were just the slightest bit ratty (a point that didn't escape Miss Baba), and extended his wing in greeting.

"Gluepots here," he said, as if he were talking to her over the telephone. "How may I be of help?" Miss Baba quickly outlined the situation concerning Harriet and Leonard's mysterious disappearance.

His feet didn't quite reach the ground...

23

Gluepots listened attentively. In fact, Miss Baba thought, if Gluepots had had any eyebrows, they would have been arching and lowering and knitting as he listened. His reaction to her story was immediate. "I can have my boat ready on an hour's notice, including my crewman, Tap Tap. Payment in advance, of course." Miss Baba waited for Gluepots to ask for a fortune and then wait for her, in return, to bargain him down. But to her gratification he gave her the price of seventy gourdes a day, which was very reasonable in that part of the world.

They sealed the bargain with a toast. Gluepots offered Miss Baba a glass of Corn Pop, which was not entirely to her liking. She sipped a bit of it so she wouldn't offend Gluepots, but it would never find its way onto her shopping list in Balston Spa.

Miss Baba mentioned to Gluepots that, before they left, she wanted to notify the police of their plans.

Gluepots, his voice deepening with concern, said, "Miss Baba, I suppose it makes sense to talk to them, but be very careful and tell them only the smallest amount of what you know. Don't mention your friend with the airplane. Don't mention that you are renting a boat. And don't tell them you're planning to look for your friends yourself."

Miss Baba thought this very peculiar. "You mean to say I shouldn't trust the police? But I should trust you, whom I've just met? And why is that?"

"Dear lady, have you ever heard of the Tontons Macoutes?"

Miss Baba thought for a second. Then she replied, "They were the national police of Haiti, a rough bunch, like pirates. But they're disbanded, aren't they?"

Gluepots attempted a smile with his stiff beak. "Their authority did not come only from the past ruler, Papa Doc, and then his son, Baby Doc. No, not by a long shot. They are part of a very proud and fierce culture—the only nation ever to have a successful slave rebellion. And these people fought trained armies, braved torture, and forced the enemy into the sea after twenty years of bloody fighting."

"Gluepots. Ah, Kernel," interrupted Miss Baba. "History is all well and good, but that was more than a hundred years ago. What does all that have to do with my going to the police?"

"Maybe nothing, maybe everything. Miss Baba, to put it bluntly,

the people whom you go to for justice might be the same people who kidnapped your friends. You know what 'Tonton Macoute' means? It means 'uncle with a shoulder bag.' Here when a child won't eat his vegetables, the mother doesn't say, 'Eat them or the bogeyman will get you.' She says, 'Eat them or the Tonton will come and take you away in his Macoute.'"

Miss Baba said impatiently, "Well, Kernel, my friends always ate their vegetables, so it couldn't be that." A moment later, she apologized for not taking his warning seriously, because there might be something to it after all. "Well, it sounds odd. You'll have to forgive me, but it's a lot to understand all at once. A country where bogeymen and wicked uncles really do exist. . . ."

The police station was not like the one in Balston Spa. It was, in fact, more like a cross between a pool hall and a pawn shop. Miss Baba asked for the officer in charge. That turned out to be Sergeant Livre Overt, the magistrate who had written the letter to Amanda and Amonya that began this whole adventure. Overt was an energetic little fellow who seemed on the level, but he said he was relatively powerless to act personally with any great success in the outer reaches of his territory. And Marmalade, the town where Leonard's baseball factory was located, happened to be very far out there in wild country.

Overt was, however, in contact with the local officer in Marmalade—a fellow by the name of Louie Lapink. Sergeant Overt

"So you are _that_ Kernel Gluepots..."

then picked up the telephone and called Lapink. As Miss Baba watched Overt squeaking animatedly into the phone, she couldn't help wondering how many books Overt had to sit on to reach the top of his desk. After the phone conversation, Overt was plainly not happy. "I thought it was a good omen, at first, that the phone actually worked. They usually do not. But I don't feel a great deal of confidence in the local authorities in that part of the country. Lapink is captain there, but there have been rumors that he is still active with the outlawed Tonton Macoute. I probably shouldn't be telling you this, but it is important to caution you, Miss Baba, not to venture out to that place. As you can see, it is possible that kidnappers are on the loose. And it is possible that you might not be able to count on the local authorities for help. Very dangerous business."

Back at the hotel, Miss Baba found Gluepots pacing in the lobby, waiting for her to return. "Ah, you are safe! Any news about your friends?"

Miss Baba recounted her adventure in the large tin shed that passed for a police station. Gluepots nodded knowingly and shrugged. "It's as I expected—maybe better than I expected. They might have fabricated some reason to put you in jail, you know."

"Really?" said Miss Baba,

surprised. "I had no idea. Oh, by the way, in your pacing, Gluepots, did you happen to see my cousin? A large, well-dressed poodle with armfuls of provisions?"

"Yes, Miss Baba, I did. However, I did not introduce myself to him as his new guide. I decided you should do the honors. He is in his room now."

They went up to Trotwood's room for a little privacy, not realizing that a somewhat suspicious, pink fellow wearing a beret and very dark glasses was listening to them. He had been standing over in the corner of the lobby, pretending to read a newspaper. And he had heard more than enough already.

Trotwood had all the gear laid out on his bed. Gluepots, after a quick introduction, looked it over approvingly. Miss Baba asked, "What's this?" She picked up a crocodile skull with all different kinds of strange things woven around it.

Trotwood replied, "I may not know Haiti, but I've been around long enough to know that when someone offers you a good luck token, you take it, whether you understand it or not. At the very least, you make the person who gave it to you happy."

Gluepots once again nodded approvingly. "Your cousin here tells me, Mr. Trotwood, that you spent a good deal of time in the tropics. Were you ever in the Sudan, by chance?"

Trot smiled. "So you are *that* Kernel Gluepots? Fantastic. Just fantastic! Baba dear, this fellow is a real hero. The Battle of Khartoum. It is an honor, sir! An honor!" Gluepots' beak blushed a bit. "That was a long time ago, but you do me honor by remembering."

"Tell me," continued Trotwood, "whatever happened to your sidekick, the one you were never without? A native chap named Tap Tap or something like that. . . ."

"Tap Tap it is, and, as you will soon see, Mr. Trotwood, he is waiting for us on my boat."

The river banks resounded with jungle noises...

4

The Forest of Crocodiles

Because of the nightly rains, the river had become swift and treacherous. The boat, *La Mouche*, went along the coast from Cap-Haitien to the mouth of the raging Limbo River. Once they left the coastal tide, they were suddenly deep within the Forest of Crocodiles. *La Mouche* groaned under the weight of the four, plus their provisions. But the boat rode well above the danger level.

When all was calm, Trotwood and Miss Baba took the occasion to get to know Tap Tap. Gluepots' assistant was a bit embarrassed that Trot knew about his past successes in North Africa and sang Tap Tap's praises.

The trip up the Limbo was uneventful, as Limbo passages go. They saw only six voodoo warnings (complete with skulls), went through two swarms of bats, avoided one whirlpool, chugged through several seebobs of man-eating perbonias, and encountered a large swimming snake that was extremely rude to them. "Where are all the crocodiles? I've only seen half a dozen in the last hour," mused Trotwood.

By late evening, they were close to their destination,

"The crocs are afraid of the perbonias," replied Gluepots. "If you don't see a croc, then you know perbonias are on the prowl. Don't put your paw in the water, unless you want a very close manicure." Gluepots wasn't kidding. He threw one of Trot's donuts over the side. It was devoured by dozens of little mouths practically before it touched the water.

They were still punting along by nightfall. The dark riverbanks resounded with jungle noises. Quite close by, they heard an unearthly sound—a deep, guttural growl followed by a shrill, bloodcurdling whistle repeated again and again.

"Zombies, I suppose," said Trotwood matter-of-factly.

"Adenoids, more likely," replied Miss Baba, looking down the throat of Tap Tap, who had fallen asleep during their long journey and was now snoring loudly. By late evening, they were close to their destination—the baseball factory near Marmalade.

the baseball factory in Marmalade...

The factory was not much by U.S. standards. In fact, it was nowhere near as big as the shoe factory in Balston Spa. But some of the world's best baseballs had come from it. And now it was all boarded up with crude hand-painted signs warning people away.

As they peered in the dusty windows, an unfamiliar voice hissed loudly, "I am Wrigley Slugfest, the foreman of this factory. What is it you desire? As you can see, the factory is closed."

Miss Baba spoke first. "I am Miss Baba Furbelow. This is Trotwood, my playboy cousin, and these are our guides, the famous military heroes Kernel Gluepots and Tap Tap. Where are Leonard and Harriet Westdale? What information do you have? What do the police have to say about all this?"

Miss Baba impatiently rattled off question after question, not really expecting answers from Slugfest, to whom she had taken an instant dislike.

Slugfest was plainly surprised to find a rescue party all the way from Balston Spa. He thought for a minute and said, "Madam, people like you find it hard to believe, but there are spirits in the forest. Spirits that are much more dangerous than the criminals and crocodiles who live there. I believe your friends are zombies. If you want to find them, you must look in the Land Without Hats. But nobody who goes there comes back."

Trotwood asked politely, "So, tell me, good fellow, where is this Land Without Hats?"

Gluepots answered before Slugfest could embark on another long-winded answer. "I'm afraid, my dear fellow, that this gentleman is telling you your friends are dead. Or living-dead. Zombies. At any rate, it's not good. Not good at all."

"As you can see, the factory is closed..."

Slugfest was encouraged by Gluepots' words. He added, "Yes, nice people, please leave this forest at once. Go home. Go far away. Leave this to the police. Or who knows what will happen to you? If you meddle in things you don't understand, maybe you will become zombies, too."

"Nonsense," said Miss Baba. "And I don't think the local police will be of much help here. Sergeant Overt in Cap-Haitien already spoke with them."

The foreman shivered. "Do not insult the crocodile mother before crossing the river," he said.

Trotwood nudged Gluepots and whispered, "Now what in blazes does he mean by that, old chap?"

Gluepots didn't answer. Instead, he cut off both Trotwood and Miss Baba. "Mister Slugfest, we don't mean to be disrespectful of your beliefs. We just want to look for our friends. Miss Baba means you no harm." While Slugfest pondered Gluepots' words, Gluepots quietly suggested to his party that they appear to leave.

They bid Slugfest farewell and retreated, but only as far as the edge of the woods, where they spent the next hour in hiding. Trot took out a pair of high-powered binoculars and waited.

While they waited, Miss Baba began to try to put the whole picture together. "Do you give any credence to all this voodoo business?" she asked Gluepots.

"Dunno," he replied. "I once saw a mountain fellow curl up and die within a week of being cursed. I'll tell you one thing, you have to be born to the belief . . . but then there are the poisons—dusts, serums, arrow potions. Those you'd best stay clear of. They'll make you very dead very quickly."

While they were talking in hushed tones, a full moon rose. They passed the binoculars back and forth. Slugfest was shovelling baseballs into the back of a jeep by the light of a kerosene lamp. "What the devil is he doing that for?" asked Trot, to no one in particular.

Another figure was with Slugfest, lurking in the shadows. He was a long-legged pink flamingo with a beret and dark glasses. A large automatic rifle was slung over one wing, and a cigarette dangled from his beak. The group overheard the two exchange greetings. "Honor," said the flamingo. "Respect," answered Slugfest. Then there were snippets of conversation about baseballs being sent to someone or other, and about the Citadel (a historic fortress Miss Baba had read about). Finally, they heard the name "Westdale" spoken. The flamingo patted Slugfest on the shell and laughed, or rather cackled.

"Wasn't that pink one at the hotel last night?" asked Miss Baba in a whisper.

Gluepots nodded. "Louie Lapink, the local police captain."

Slugfest finally extinguished his lamp and flung his shovel into the woods. Then he and Lapink drove off.

It didn't take long for the group to decide to follow him, instead of inspecting the factory.

The countryside slipped by quickly in the night ...

5

The Citadel

The rescuers set off on foot after Slugfest's jeep. The concrete road, like most of the roads on the island, was full of gigantic potholes, so the jeep couldn't go much faster than the speed of a brisk walk. Meanwhile, Miss Baba noticed a railroad track running alongside the road. The rail bed was gravel, which made walking less like going through an obstacle course. So, they followed the tracks.

As luck would have it, they found a small handcar. Miss Baba was delighted. "A handcar! Unless the tracks are ripped up, we'll certainly make better time than Slugfest." Trotwood, at this point, was also quite content to give a blister on his foot some rest, too.

From then on, as Gluepots would say, it was smooth sailing. The countryside slipped by quickly in the night. Miss Baba shined a lantern ahead of the handcar to make sure they didn't hit anything, as she also kept an eye on Slugfest's headlights.

Finally, the jeep turned off the road and stopped at the base of the huge, crumbling fortress called the Citadel.

"There is a little-known treacherous path..."

The handcar slowed to a noiseless halt not too far away. The four rescuers left it on a siding near the base of the fortress and approached the jeep through the bushes. They watched Slugfest leave the vehicle and Lapink behind and prepare to climb the main path to the summit of the Citadel.

"Ah, it is possible for us to get to the summit a good half hour before he does," said Gluepots, clearly enjoying the chase.

Trotwood and Tap Tap caught their breath after pumping the handcar. "There is a little-known treacherous path," said Gluepots. Miss Baba asked, "Just how treacherous is this secret path you have in mind? After all, you have wings, and we don't."

"My dear lady, my plan is for us to ride up on Tap Tap. He is incredibly surefooted. He's beaten mountain goats up the sheer side of K2 for sport. You will be quite safe on his back." Gluepots' words certainly had a calming effect.

Astride Tap Tap, however, Miss Baba found little to take comfort in. They traversed narrow, winding ledges with sheer walls on one side and dizzying drops on the other, all by the light of the moon. "Touch the wall," whispered Kernel Gluepots, "and you will feel less afraid."

After about an hour of this, they reached the top. "Thank you for the lift, Tap Tap, old chap," said Trotwood. Gluepots peered over

36

the cliff, checked his watch, and pronounced that they had made good time. "Slugfest is still only halfway up. We have at least thirty minutes. He'll arrive by two a.m., as I figured."

They turned to the fortress and Trotwood exclaimed, "Machu Picchu in Peru, the palaces in the mountain passes of Tibet, and the strongholds in the Atlas Mountains. I've seen them all, and this Citadel is unquestionably one of the world's greatest sights."

"That's not much comfort to the eighteen thousand slaves who died building it," said Gluepots.

They pressed on to the great iron doors barring the Citadel. A large, ornate key, gray-brown with rust and recent oil, was hanging on a nail stuck between two of the stones in the wall near the door. Trotwood fit the key into the lock. It turned and the door swung open. "Since the key was easy to find, we might conclude that the purpose of locking the door was to keep people in, not out," he said.

The enormous iron door opened with a deep groan. Trot put the key back where he found it and pushed the door closed in hopes that Slugfest wouldn't notice it had been tampered with.

Miss Baba was already exploring the large open courtyard of the fortress. It appeared deserted to her. Then, over in a far corner next to a huge pile of rusted cannonballs, she saw two forms.

"Harriet? Leonard?" called out Miss Baba. There was no reply.

Miss Baba, Trot, Gluepots, and Tap Tap stood in front of the two. They were indeed Harriet and Leonard, but there was something ghastly about their faces. They turned their heads as if they were windup toys.

"Leonard, old bean, we were scared silly about you two! We thought you might be dead!" cried out Trotwood, delighted to see them alive. Leonard mumbled something, forcing Trot to lean close to hear.

"What did they say?" an anxious Miss Baba asked.

"I believe," Trot replied, "if I'm not mistaken, Leonard said 'glurp, glurpglurp.' Is that some sort of local dialect? Sounds like gibberish to me."

Gluepots and Tap Tap glanced at each other. They knew exactly what the matter was. "Zombies," said Kernel Gluepots. "Someone has given these two the beastly zombie poison. They are experiencing a run-in with a very dangerous drug. It is derived from the crapaud toad and puffer fish, the most deadly poisons known. In

37

small doses, this stuff makes people into the frightfully boring creatures you see here."

"Well, that won't do at all!" said Trotwood, outraged that someone would do this to Harriet and Leonard. "They were such a charming couple. They danced beautifully, engaged in clever repartee, knew the best foods, and always served magnificent desserts! There must be something we can do! . . . Say, come to think of it, isn't crapaud what I had for dinner last night? That— what did you call it—the most deadly poison known?"

Gluepots corrected Trotwood. "Not to worry, my dear Trotwood. The flesh of the crapaud is a delicacy here. The poison glands are carefully removed before it is cooked. Although mistakes have been known to happen. . . ."

Crapaud

Tap Tap was rummaging around in his pockets. He pulled out a very strange thing. It was about the size and shape of a cucumber, but it had long, rubbery tendrils, like thick hairs, sticking out every which way. Tap Tap was very careful not to puncture the skin of this thing with his teeth. He passed it to Gluepots, who took it very carefully.

"As luck would have it," said Gluepots, responding to the inquisitive stares of Miss Baba and Trot, "Tap Tap is familiar with

38

the plants and herbs of this island. He suspected that there might be some zombie trouble."

"But what is this green thing?" asked Miss Baba.

"The wild cucumber," replied Gluepots. "The Indians of your country used it to commit suicide. It is a deadly poison. But in the proper amount, used correctly, it is the only known antidote for zombie poison."

As they were beginning to prepare the poisonous "bearded cucumber," they heard the key in the lock of the Citadel gate. "Slugfest is here," whispered Gluepots.

Harriet and Leonard let out a "glurp."

"Leave them here," said Gluepots. "Let's see what he's up to." The four rescuers quietly moved into the shadows.

Wild Cucumber

"If you were people, you could have walked right out..."

6

Land Without Hats

The voice of Wrigley Slugfest rasped across the Citadel courtyard. It was no longer the polite voice the rescuers had encountered earlier that evening. "Hey, you zombies!" he shouted at Harriet and Leonard. "It's a good thing you're zombies. Your old buddy Mr. Slugfest must have forgotten to lock the gate. If you were people, you could have walked right out." He laughed loudly and walked toward the prisoners. "Hey, you two, take off all your jewelry—your wristwatches, earrings, rings. That's good. Now put them in this bag. Good!"

In one hand, Slugfest had a sack, in the other he held a gun pointed at Harriet and Leonard, just in case they weren't perfectly zombified. After he collected the jewelry, the foreman laughed again and said, "There's going to be a little spontaneous combustion at the factory tonight! These trinkets should be enough to convince everybody that you're goners—which will be true in a week or two." He walked back to the gate and then said, over his shoulder, "But just to be sure, I'm gonna lock up well this time and leave the key with the fishes at the bottom of the cliff."

They heard the key in the door, then a faint grunt as Slugfest lobbed the key out over the water.

Miss Baba was first to speak. "Gluepots, is there any other way out of this place besides the front gate?"

"I don't think there is, except for straight up" was the reply.

About an hour after Tap Tap had carefully prepared and

41

administered the antidote to the zombie poison, Harriet and Leonard were more or less recovered. "You don't know what it's like!" cried Harriet. "You can hear and see what's going on, but you're powerless to do anything about it. Why, yesterday I had a terrible itch on my nose, but I couldn't manage to scratch it!"

Leonard was still suffering from a headache, but managed to say, "Why on earth did he do this to us? We discovered he was stealing some baseballs. But the worst thing we would have done was dismiss him. What he took wasn't very valuable, after all."

Trotwood, meanwhile, was having a quandary of his own. "Why didn't I think of posting one of us outside the wall?"

Gluepots was hardly any cheerier. "Remember the Land Without Hats? Well, that's where we'll wind up unless we think of something within a day or two, tops." Harriet began to cry.

Miss Baba sensed it was time for someone to take charge. "What we must do," she said, "is to put our heads together, with or without hats, and find a way out. Now we're in this huge cone, one hundred feet high at least, wouldn't you say?"

Tap Tap quietly corrected her: "One hundred and thirty-two."

"Thank you, one hundred and thirty-two, and the top is open. So we could think of ways to scale these sheer walls. Tap Tap, are there any weak spots in the wall, any holes, cracks, anything we can squeeze through?"

Tap Tap shook his head no. "Not even the mice find ways through these walls. They're very well engineered."

"Couldn't you fly out the top to get help?" Miss Baba said to Kernel Gluepots.

"Impossible . . . impossible!" blurted out the Kernel, his beak blushing slightly. "Never fly, never fly, navy man." Miss Baba didn't press the issue—after all, Gluepots was probably too bottom-heavy to fly, she thought.

Trotwood suggested a meal might help them, or at least him, to think more clearly. So, huddled together, they collected the few scraps they had. Miss Baba took off her egg and cut it into six rather meager slices. Trotwood fished around in his pockets and found some Beezer Bits and an eyepatch made from a special Albany licorice, never used. Tap Tap threw an apple onto the pile, and Gluepots pulled out a small bag of rhubarb-flavored jelly beans, something the veteran explorer would never be without.

As if things weren't bad enough, just then the wind rose and a driving rain followed, obscuring the full moon. The high walls sheltered them a little from the rain, but not much. As their eyes adjusted to the dim light, they took stock of their surroundings. A bare stone floor, a few rusty cannonballs, some old fishing nets. There was a tiny barred window on the massive door, but even without the bars, it would have been too small for any of them to squeeze through.

After the meal Trotwood pulled out his pipe. The bubbles soothed his troubled mind and his upset stomach.

"Trotwood, how high will your bubbles fly before they burst?" Miss Baba asked.

"How high?" answered Trot. "Well, let's see. It just so happens I can tell you that. Given the proper air conditions, of course. Dr. Pignewton and I tested this particular blend to the rather spectacular height of twelve thousand feet. Some of them went higher, but we settled on that as a predictable number."

"Couldn't you SOS with those bubbles, Trot?" asked Miss Baba excitedly. "Maybe someone will see it. It's our only hope."

"Why, I believe I could at that!" Trotwood readied his pipe, a precision model. This pipe was handcrafted for Trot by Lars Wedgeworth in the town of Spitz, Norway. In the hands of a master, it was a thing to be reckoned with. Trotwood could put a bubble through the eye of a needle at fifty paces.

As he put his pipe to his lips, the smile of an artist absorbed in his work flashed across his square jaw. First, three long bubbles, then three short ones, then three long. A test. Then three long bubbles of immense proportion, then three huge short bubbles, then three long ones again.

They wobbled up above the walls of the Citadel, caught the bright light of the full moon, and drifted off in long thin sequences toward the northwest and Tortuga Island.

Miss Baba, too damp to nap, sat on a rusty cannonball and watched the bubbles continue to rise in a stream, shimmering in the moonlight. They rose above the walls of the Citadel and blew off to the west at a fast pace.

Miss Baba, too damp to nap, sat on a rusty cannonball ...

7

Trotwood Uses His Noodle

It was a beautiful display of bubble blowing, everyone agreed. But if they were the only ones to see it, it would be all for nothing. Trotwood sat in the middle of the courtyard under a patch of moonlight. He was thinking about an experiment that he and Dr. Pignewton had done just a month or two earlier.

"That's it," he said to himself. "Pignewton's theory of bubble density."

He gathered up some scrap wood and started a small camp fire. Then he took the cap off the silver flask that contained the bubble mix and attached a handle made of old wire and a stick. He held the flask over the fire and heated the mix, being careful not to let it boil. When he was satisfied with the consistency, he blew one test bubble. As it hung in the air, he poked it with a stick. When he hit it, it sailed across the yard, struck a wall, and bounced back.

Sure enough, the net started to rise...

"Actually, I've never seen one that strong. Maybe it interacted with the silver of the canister when I heated it," thought Trot. He asked everyone to collect the old fishing nets and tie the sound ones together. Trot instructed everyone to stand on the bottom net. Leonard tied the last knot and Trotwood proceeded to blow hundreds of large, tough-as-nails bubbles.

The nets strained, the old ropes creaked under the rising bubbles. One or two strands broke from the weight of the passengers, but the rest of the nets held tight.

As they rose through the cone of the Citadel, Miss Baba looked at the moss-covered walls. She realized that probably no one had looked closely at these stones since Henri Christophe's slave laborers took down their scaffolding one hundred and sixty years earlier.

Soon the six captives could see over the top of the wall and could feel the wind blowing toward Tortuga and freedom.

The bubbles accumulated in the net, joining to make larger and larger bubbles. And, as the net rose above the walls of the prison, the bubbles became iridescent with moonlight.

Harriet exclaimed, "A hot-air balloon! How delightful!" Trotwood found nothing delightful in the thought that Harriet had just said he was full of hot air.

They easily cleared the wall. To the north, the moon glinted off the ocean. The countryside beneath them was mostly shrouded in shadows. The escapees could pick out large things in the moonlight— mountains, valleys, and rivers—but not a light was to be seen. The world was asleep except for the six in the net.

Trotwood, to begin the descent, tapped a hole in one of the bubbles with a hammer and a very sharp pin. "POP!" it broke. But then, something unexpected happened. "POP!" Another bubble burst by itself. Then, "POP! POP! POP!"

Trotwood was perplexed. What could be causing these virtually indestructible bubbles to break? "Tap Tap, old boy, you know something of chemistry. What's your opinion?"

Tap Tap cleared his throat and thought, "Well, you said the silver of your canister might have made the bubbles stronger. Maybe something about the silver is causing them to pop unexpectedly. Maybe the air pressure or temperature or exposure to moonlight has made your solution unstable."

By now they were falling at an alarming rate of speed. Bubbles were popping left and right, and the earth was looming closer.

They easily cleared the wall...

47

And all of them were plummeting to earth . . .

8

Just Desserts

It was definitely one of the strangest sights ever seen in the skies over Haiti (which is saying a lot): a net containing two well-dressed poodles, a military sort of goose and donkey, and a rather furry factory owner and his wife. And all of them were plummeting to earth.

Kernel Gluepots put his wings through the mesh of the net and began to flap with all his might. Leonard noticed a slight slowing down of their fall. But it wasn't enough.

Everyone was screaming suggestions or commenting on someone else's suggestions—all at the same time. Meanwhile, they were about to experience what could easily be the world's roughest balloon landing on record.

They were making such a racket that they all failed to notice a distant hum which was growing closer. They also failed to notice a glint of silver in the dawning sun.

Suddenly their fall stopped in mid-air at less than a thousand feet. The few remaining bubbles burst, and, after a violent bounce, the net actually started to rise. When the contents of the net

Suddenly their fall stopped in mid-air ...

regained their wits a little, they realized there was a deafening roar above them. It was the unmistakable noise of a well-tuned, 260-horse-power deHavilland engine, the kind normally found in a Tiger Moth.

As the addled brains of the six adventurers sorted out the facts, Hairy Martha activated the electric winch and hoisted them into the cargo bay of the airplane. Once inside, Martha helped them out of the net. Then she offered them some very welcome cups of hot cocoa. (Actually, it was the last of the cocoa Miss Baba had brought along for the flight to Haiti.) In her dazed condition, Miss Baba thought how, just last Sunday morning, she had been sitting on the back porch reading about edible hats when Martha had hit the foul ball. She felt the top of her head and recalled they had eaten her hat the previous night. She had a twinge of indigestion remembering the rhubarb jelly beans and then closed her eyes and took a well-deserved nap.

When they landed at the Tortuga airstrip, Fly-Girl Betty and Hairy Martha exchanged hugs and handshakes all around.

"I got your SOS," said Betty, "but I couldn't take off in the storm. As soon as it blew over, we left. Just in time, I'd say."

The next item on the agenda was to bring Slugfest to justice. There was no telephone at the airstrip, so Miss Baba called Cap-

Haitien on the Tiger Moth's radio. She finally got through to Sergeant Livre Overt. "Bonjour, Sergeant!" blasted Miss Baba.

"Madame Baba? It is you!" he squeaked. "I was so worried. Are you well? And your friends?"

"Oui, oui! All is well, Sergeant. We found our friends. They are now safe. But an attempt was made on our lives by the factory's foreman, Wrigley Slugfest, and your police captain out there, Louie Lapink."

There was a pause on the other end of the line, then, "Wrigley Slugfest and that no-good Louie Lapink. I have been trying to develop a case against them for years. Ah, but I kept hoping Lapink was honest even though he was nasty. I will put out an all-points bulletin for the turtle with a ship tattoo and an off-center fang, and a shifty-looking flamingo with a tobacco-stained beak."

"Sergeant Overt, there is one more question. Why baseballs?"

"Miss Baba, perhaps we should continue this conversation on a more private basis," suggested Overt. "Anyone could be listening to this radio frequency! But I must tell you one more thing. Inspector Lechien, whom I believe you know, is working with me on this case. I expect a speedy capture."

Miss Baba did indeed know the renowned Inspector Lechien, famous for his brilliant solution of the Case of the Four Soup Bones.

The group took a launch back to the mainland. (Trotwood thought they said "lunch.") Betty and Martha accompanied them since the Tiger Moth was in perfect running condition and their friends were still a little shaky from their experiment with bubble flying.

At the hotel, they partook of a sumptuous feast of everything on the menu—except for the crapaud, which Trot discreetly asked to be omitted. Nevertheless, he inspected his seafood casserole for bizarre creatures before he dug in.

Miss Baba had the chef whip up Trotwood's favorite desserts— all of them. The waiters carried out trays of blueberry pie sandwiches, donuts in flaming brandy, and chocolate pudding omelets. Gluepots, who had never encountered the last item, remarked to Tap Tap, "After a chocolate pudding omelet, I'm not so sure a toad in cream sauce is all that repulsive." Tap Tap nodded in agreement, remembering times when stranger creatures than toads had wandered into their cooking pots when the two were in the steamy jungles of New Guinea.

After dinner, they watched the floor show, the famous Flamingo

After dinner, they watched the floor show...

Dancers doing the merengue. It was well past Martha's bedtime, but Miss Baba let her stay up just this once to celebrate. Martha did her best to keep her eyes from closing during the dance act. But the swirls of pink feathers and long legs gave way to dreams about being home and hitting more long balls—this time to the outfield, not the neighbors' window.

The words to the merengue drifted softly through her half-sleep . . .

> "Goodbye, my friends, goodbye,
> We all live on one earth together,
> We all enjoy the same sun and water, winds and
>   mountains, plants and animals.
> Why, my brothers, are we so far and so close?
> Goodbye, my friends, goodbye."

Meanwhile, at the table, talk turned to what Harriet and Leonard planned to do. "There's no reason to stay here now, what with the baseball factory burned down," said Leonard. "Besides, it would be good to see Balston Spa again. Betty, you don't think you might have room on the Tiger Moth for me and Harriet?"

Fly-Girl Betty had no objection. On Tortuga, Hairy Martha had come up with the idea of installing wing tanks for gasoline on the Tiger Moth. So there was a good deal more cabin space available now, even after packing Miss Baba's six aluminum suitcases (made by Haitian craftsmen from old soup cans) full of fine native cocoa from Jeremie.

"In fact, we have room for another two passengers," added Betty. "Even one with hooves."

Kernel Gluepots and Tap Tap, realizing this was an invitation, smiled. "Well, a trip north. It's been years since we've seen the States, hasn't it, Tap Tap?"

"Eight years, Kernel."

"Well, that's time enough. What say we visit this Balston Spa?" That settled it. While everyone packed the following day, the old *La Mouche* was brought down river and stored in mothballs.

Meanwhile, the authorities, under the supervision of Sergeant Overt and Inspector Lechien, gave chase to the diabolical foreman Slugfest and his Tonton Macoute henchman Louie Lapink. That morning, a patrol intercepted them in Slugfest's jeep, piled high with contraband baseballs. They were chased to the cliffs along the coast, where Slugfest lost control of his vehicle.

The two just barely jumped clear as the jeep went over the cliff and plummeted into the deep water below. The jeep and the baseballs would never be recovered, but Slugfest and Lapink were in custody, rather the worse for wear. The Sergeant took lengthy depositions from all involved, and only then permitted the rescuers to leave the country. In fact, he *insisted* that they leave, since Lapink had a lot of dangerous associates who wouldn't like the idea of his going to jail for ten to twenty years. Slugfest, who had actually done the kidnapping, was bound to get even more, according to the Sergeant.

Just before leaving the police station, Miss Baba stopped in the office of Inspector Lechien. "Why, Meeez Baba," he exclaimed. "When I arrived from France, I was told that a charming American poodle from Balston Spa had rescued the Westdale couple. Of course, I am not surprised to find it was you. As always, I offer you a position with Interpol, the international police agency, any time you like."

Miss Baba had always found Lechien to embody everything good about the French. Even the little cleft in his chin was charming. "Ah, Inspector, you're too generous. But even if I were worthy of your offer, I should have to decline it. I am an educator, you know."

Lechien kissed her paw and bowed. "We will meet again," he said.

The Tiger Moth landed in the late afternoon...

9

Safe at Home

The Tiger Moth landed late in the afternoon on the back lawn of the Academy. The foundlings had put together an impromptu band and hung banners and balloons all over the grounds. A holiday was declared.

The Teasedale sisters came running over through the hedgerow. Harriet and Leonard disembarked first, to a round of applause and big kisses from Harriet's weeping sisters. Then came Miss Baba and Trotwood, to another round of cheers. When Kernel Gluepots and Tap Tap stepped down, Miss Baba introduced them to a roaring crowd.

Last off the plane were the crew, Fly-Girl Betty and Hairy Martha. The ovation for this tired duo was as loud as any of the others.

The kids crowded around Martha. They put her on their shoulders and carried her around in her pilot's coveralls and cap.

After the group was filled in on all the details of the rescue, Trot and Miss Baba accompanied the Teasedales and Westdales back to Overlook for a cup of cocoa.

"What I still don't understand is why Slugfest and Lapink resorted to theft and kidnapping over something as insignificant as a few hundred baseballs," mused Leonard. "They weren't that valuable."

All of a sudden, they heard a "CRASH!" Another ball sailed through the recently repaired window at Overlook. It rolled to a stop at the feet of the guests having cocoa. The glass had cut the stitching of the ball, which had unraveled all over the floor. Instead of a rubber core, this ball had a shiny golden center.

Trotwood peeled the skin back further and pulled out a medallion bearing the seal of the King of Spain and a date, 1492. "This appears to be pirate treasure, unless Harriet is in the habit of keeping her jewelry in baseballs," he said.

Miss Baba turned the medal in her paw. "I believe this was the property of Christopher Columbus. Could this be from the wreck of the *Santa Maria*? Why, this is extraordinary!"

Gluepots became excited. "Why, I believe you're right! The *Santa Maria* was lost in a storm off the coast of Tortuga Island!"

The children collected all the balls Leonard and Harriet had sent from Haiti. When they had peeled away the leather, they had a treasure trove of gold and gems.

"Slugfest and Lapink may have plundered any number of wrecks off the coast of Tortuga," suggested Gluepots. "It used to be a pirate stronghold. Those wrecks are protected by the government.

Santa Maria
Piece of eight   Medallion   Crusado   Dubloon

Salvage crews are supposed to have permits and give whatever treasure they find to the government." Gluepots knew his stuff.

After two hours of trying to get a call through to Inspector Lechien, Miss Baba finally reached him. "Monsieur! I have news! Before the kidnapping, Leonard and Harriet sent a crate of baseballs to Overlook. Those baseballs contain artifacts from Christopher Columbus and the *Santa Maria*."

"Ah, yes," said the Inspector. "I was beginning to suspect as much. But until now, we could not recover any evidence from the bottom of the ocean and we could prove nothing. Your crate of baseballs will make our case. And the National Museum director will be very happy."

Back at the Academy, Miss Baba confronted a very uncomfortable looking Hairy Martha, who stood waiting, bat in paw. "The guilty party, I presume? Martha, we'll have to have the gardener turn the baseball diamond around so this doesn't happen anymore. But I really don't think you're in trouble. Your foul ball just happened to solve the case . . . though I think, for now, you should practice croquet. Trotwood is a world-class player and can give you some pointers." (Several of the young Pointers in the group giggled.)

"As they say in Haiti, 'Bon Dieu bon,'" said Kernel Gluepots. "Things will work out for the best."

"Monsieur, I have news . . ."

57

Extra Innings

A few months later, things sorted themselves out. Miss Baba had had a little time to reflect on the episode. Everything did, after all, turn out for the best (bon Dieu bon, as Gluepots was now fond of saying).

The Kernel and Tap Tap decided to stay in Balston Spa for the time being. They sold their boat in Haiti and opened a catering company called "Mrs. Gluepots" in honor of Gluepots' mother who, apparently, was a pretty good cook.

Leonard and Harriet Westdale received a tidy sum of money from the insurance on the baseball factory. But they had had enough of baseballs. They decided instead to start a company that manufactured croquet balls. "At least they're solid," said Leonard on more than one occasion.

Hairy Martha was offered a contract with a top minor league baseball team, but she decided to go to college before she went pro. She also became an inventor and has already patented a machine that repairs broken windows automatically. Sales are brisk.

Miss Baba, meanwhile, became absorbed in choosing one of several very special recipes from Animal Maria. She wanted an especially beautiful and delicious cake for an upcoming birthday party. Little did she know that this simple domestic venture would turn into an international adventure—eventually taking the entire Academy to the volcanic mountains of Mongolia in search of "The Doorknob of Destiny."

Glossary

Atlas Mountains: A mountain range in northwest Africa extending from Morocco to Tunisia. Trotwood's been there.

Balston Spa: A quiet, little town located on the Mohawk River (see James Fenimore Cooper's *Leatherstocking Tales*). It's between Albany, the capital of New York state, and Saratoga Springs, where Diamond Jim Brady used to spend his summers. It is also a spa—a place people visit to take mineral baths that are supposed to be good for them.

"Baby Doc" Duvalier: Born in 1951; President (dictator) of Haiti from 1971 to 1986. He inherited Haiti from his father, Papa Doc. In 1986, Baby Doc (Jean-Claude) went into voluntary exile. Today he lives somewhere in Europe and is very rich, unlike his former countrymen—who are, for the most part, very poor.

Bon Dieu Bon: A Haitian expression meaning "things will work out for the best." The literal translation is "the good God is good."

Cap-Haitien: The northernmost city in Haiti. It's known for having mostly stone structures, built after the city was burned down in the early 1800s.

Cheesequake State Park: Located in eastern New Jersey. Years ago, this was the site of some low-intensity earthquakes. Why the park was named Cheesequake, however, is not entirely clear.

Henri Christophe: One of the great leaders of the Haitian revolution in the early 1800s. Unfortunately, Christophe turned into a ruthless tyrant, crowned himself king, and turned his people into slaves again. He finally killed himself with a golden bullet.

The Citadel: A spectacular fortress in the north of Haiti. The Citadel was built for Henri Christophe by tens of thousands of slaves, many of whom lost their lives in the process.

Crapaud: A Haitian toad that grows to as much as two pounds in weight and six inches in length. It has poison glands on its back that are (very carefully) removed prior to cooking. The crapaud is a popular food in Haiti.

Gourde: The currency of Haiti. It's worth about twenty cents in American money.

Haiti: Located on the island of Hispaniola, between Cuba and Puerto Rico. Haiti is a wonderful and mysterious country that Americans fall in love with when they visit. Its capital city, Port-au-Prince, is on the west coast of the island. Haiti means "land of mountains" in a native Indian language. It has had its share of misfortunes, but soon, hopefully, "bon Dieu bon."

Honor/Respect: A polite greeting in Haiti. It is similar to the American greeting, "How are you?/Fine, thank you."

K2:   The second highest mountain in the world. K2 is located in Kashmir, which is either in India or Pakistan (the ownership is disputed). Tap Tap climbed the peak. Trotwood's been there, too, although he didn't go all the way up.

Khartoum: The capital city of Sudan in North Africa. It's located where the White and Blue Nile rivers join. Trotwood's been there. This is where Gluepots and Tap Tap distinguished themselves.

Land Without Hats: The afterworld. To those who practice the Voodoo religion, this is the place people go when they die, before they go to heaven or hell.

Machu Picchu: The remains of an ancient Inca city in the mountains of Peru. Trotwood's been there.

Maître D': Headwaiter, as in a restaurant. This French term is short for maître d'hôtel.

Merengue: A popular native dance of Haiti that is energetic and graceful. It has roots in both African and European dances of the 1700s.

Santa Maria: Christopher Columbus' flagship for his voyage in 1492 when he discovered the New World. It sank off Tortuga in Haiti.

Seebobs of Perbonias: Gluepots' pet term for schools of voracious freshwater needlefish.

Solenodon: A foot-long insect-eating rodent with a long, hairy snout. He is native to the island of Hispaniola, where Haiti is.

Tap Tap: The name of one of our heroes; also, what Haitians call a taxi. It's been said that taxis got this name because, after a while, all their engines make that sound.

Tiger Moth: A plucky little airplane named after a moth that has stripes on its wings. Pilots have been flying them since the end of World War I, seventy years ago, and they still enjoy flying them. Today, they're used mostly by stunt pilots and by old airplane collectors.

Tonton Macoute: A Haitian French term meaning "uncle with a sack over his shoulder." He's like the bogeyman, who's supposed to carry off naughty children. It's also the name of Papa Doc and Baby Doc's secret police force, who carried off a lot of Haitian citizens, naughty or not.

Tortuga Island: An island off the coast of northern Haiti. It once was a pirate stronghold. Many wrecked ships (such as the *Santa Maria*) are in the waters off the island, and it's rumored that pirate treasure is still buried on the island.

Viscount Melville Sound: A water inlet so far north that it's actually inside the Arctic Circle. It's so out of the way, it isn't even in a time zone—which makes it impossible to set your watch there. Trotwood fishes here on occasion.

Voodoo: The traditional religion of the Haitian people. The proper name for it in Haiti is Vodoun.

Zombies: People who are neither dead nor alive. In the Voodoo religion, these are people who have lost their will and are slaves of those who made them zombies. Recent evidence suggests that this is accomplished with powerful drugs extracted from native toads and blowfish. These drugs act on people who believe they are possessed, not just poisoned. The use of these drugs is outlawed in modern-day Haiti.

For Miss Baba and all her friends,
and for Jarold Ramsey.

A portion of the proceeds from the
sale of this book is donated to the
children of Haiti.

Winslow Pinney Pels is a graduate of Skidmore College and lives with her
husband and son in Pound Ridge, New York.

Richard Pels is a vice president of a New York advertising agency. He has a
B.A. from the University of Rochester and an M.F.A. in Creative Writing from
the University of Oregon. Richard is also a published poet.

Miss Baba Furbelow

Animal Maria

Nurse Pincher

Hairy Martha

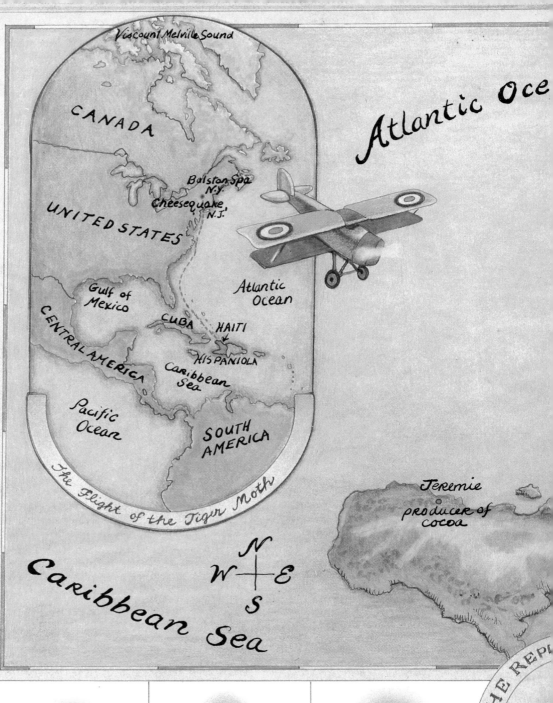

Viscount Melville Sound

Atlantic Oce

CANADA

UNITED STATES

Balston Spa
N.Y.
Cheesequake,
N.J.

Atlantic
Ocean

Gulf of
Mexico

CENTRAL AMERICA

CUBA

HAITI

HISPANIOLA

Caribbean
Sea

Pacific
Ocean

SOUTH
AMERICA

The Flight of the Tiger Moth

Caribbean Sea

N
W E
S

Jeremie
producer of
cocoa

THE REPU

Amanda

Amanya

Harriet & Leonard